SOME DADS

First published as *Some Dads* by Scholastic Press
a division of Scholastic Australia Pty Limited in 2011
This edition published under licence from Scholastic Australia Pty Limited
First Running Press Kids edition, 2017

Published by Running Press Kids,
An Imprint of Perseus Books, LLC,
A Subsidiary of Hachette Book Group, Inc.

Printed in Canada
FRI

Books published by Running Press are available at special discounts for bulk
purchases in the United States by corporations, institutions, and other organizations.
For more information, please contact the Special Markets Department at Perseus Books,
2300 Chestnut Street, Suite 200, Philadelphia, PA 19103, or call (800) 810-4145, ext. 5000,
or e-mail special.markets@perseusbooks.com.

ISBN 978-0-7624-6199-8
Library of Congress Control Number: 2016945285

9 8 7 6 5 4 3 2
Digit on the right indicates the number of this printing

Typography: Euphorigenic and Geist Serifa

Running Press Book Publishers
2300 Chestnut Street
Philadelphia, PA 19103–4371

Visit us on the web!
www.runningpress.com/rpkids

SOME DADS

nick bland

RP|KIDS
PHILADELPHIA

There are some dads who **worry**.

And some dads who

hurry.

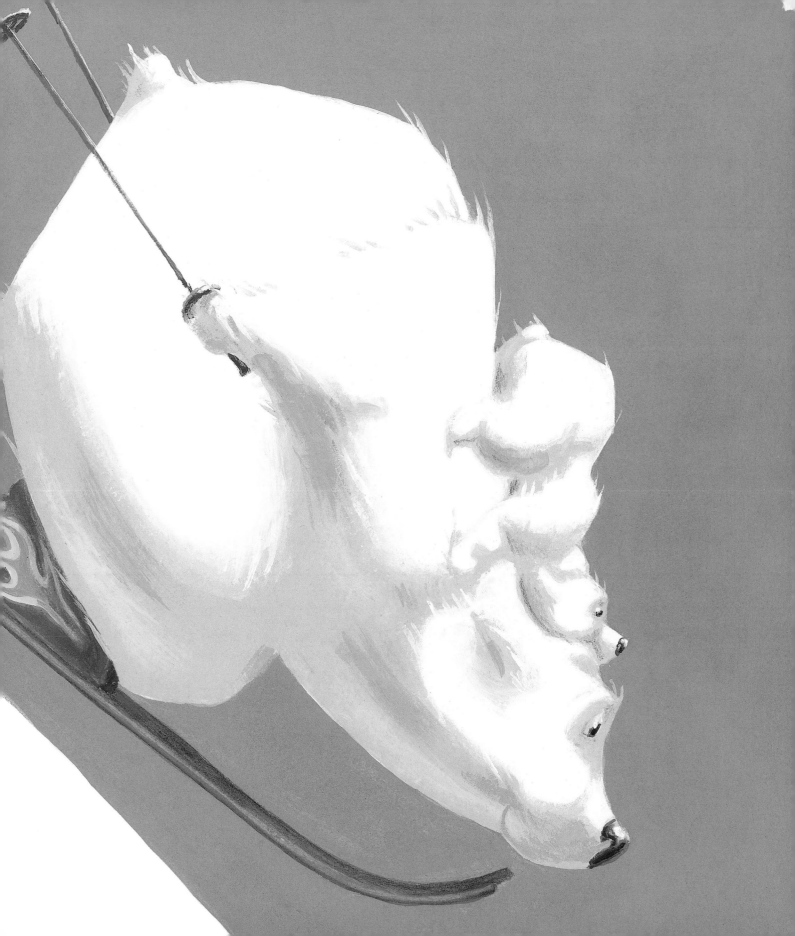

And some dads who get lost on the way.

Some dads are **sporty**.

And some dads are naughty.

And some dads just brighten your day.

Some dads like **strolling**.

And some dads

rock 'n' rolling.

And some dads just love the outdoors.

Some dads are
loud.

And all dads are
proud.

And you'll never forget
which is yours.